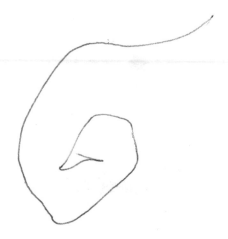

A Gift for

_____

from

_____

_____

_____ 19 _____

Art Director: Tricia Legault

Designer: Joseph Hernandez

© 1994 by The Lyons Group

End sheet photo by de Wys/Sipa/Burlet

A Division of The Lyons Group

300 East Bethany Drive, Allen, Texas 75002

Barney™, Baby Bop™ and BJ™ are trademarks of The Lyons Group

1 2 3 4 5 6 7 8 9 10   96 95 94

ISBN 1-57064-028-9

Library of Congress Number 94-70569

Based on a story by
Dennis DeShazer, Sheryl Leach
Kathy Parker, Stephen White

Illustrated by
Jay B. Johnson

One very special night, Tosha had two friends in her bedroom. One was her friend Min and the other was her favorite toy dinosaur, Barney. Tosha's mother was reading a bedtime story to the girls about a ship that sailed to Imagination Island.

4

"It's Barney!" Min and Tosha shouted happily.

In a burst of colorful sparkles, the little toy dinosaur had turned into a great big friend who gave great big hugs.

"Hi, Tosha! Hello, Min!" Barney laughed. "I sure like your story about the ship that sails to Imagination Island."

"I'd love to ride on a ship like that," said Min.

"Maybe you can," said Barney, "if we all use our imaginations!"

Tosha and Min looked at the
book and tried to imagine an
adventure on a ship. Suddenly,
sparkles of light flew out of Tosha's
book and into her closet.

"I think something fun is
starting to happen!" Barney
whispered.

The girls watched as a stairway appeared in the closet. Barney climbed the stairs, then called back to his friends.

"Come on up," Barney said. "You won't believe this!"

Tosha and Min climbed the stairs and opened a small door.

"It's a ship!" said Tosha.

"Just like the one in your book," said Min.

And it was! They were all standing on a very big wooden ship that rocked gently from side to side as it sailed through the ocean's waves. Min and Tosha pointed up at the large sails that flapped in the warm and wonderful wind.

When Min and Tosha looked down from the sails, they got another surprise.

"Look!" said Tosha. "Our clothes have changed."

"That's right," laughed Barney, who was dressed like a sea captain. "We've got a fine ship and a good wind in our sails. I think we're all ready for a fun adventure at sea."

"I like to have fun," said a happy little voice. "I want to play, too!"

Min and Tosha were surprised to see their friend Baby Bop climbing out of a tiny doorway carrying her favorite yellow blankey.

But before they could say hello, they heard somebody whistling.

"It's my big brother, BJ!" said Baby Bop.

"That's me!" laughed BJ as he climbed down a rope and joined his sister. "We have a few more friends hiding on this ship too!"

Everyone started looking around the big ship.

"This is like hide and seek," Baby Bop giggled.

After lots of looking, they found Shawn hiding in a barrel and Derek behind the ship's big steering wheel.

"Oh, good," said Barney. "We have lots of friends to have fun with now. And we're all on our way to Imagination Island!"

The ship sailed for a long time. When Imagination Island was getting close, there was a flash of lightning and a BOOM of thunder!

"Oh, no!" said Tosha. "It's a storm—just like in the book!"

Rain started to fall and the ship was rocked by bigger and bigger waves.

The waves made the ship go up and down so fast it was
hard to stand up.

Barney said, "This is a strong ship. We'll all be fine."

Then BJ called out, "Here comes a super giant wave!"

"Hold on, everybody!" said Barney.

The wave made a loud roaring sound as it hit the ship and
lifted it high into the air.

Suddenly the ship stopped rocking.

"That's good," said Min. "Maybe the storm is over."

"There's no more rain," said Derek. "And the clouds are leaving, too!"

"Gee, now the island looks really close," said Shawn.

Barney peeked over the side of the ship and got a big surprise.

"That's because we're **on** the island!" he laughed. "Or at least, above it!"

And they were! The big wave had lifted the whole ship into the tops of some palm trees and left it there safe and sound.

Baby Bop found a rope ladder and everyone climbed down to the sandy beach.

"I don't think we can get the ship down from the trees without help," said Barney.

"Then what can we do?" asked Tosha.

"We can go exploring," said Barney.

"BJ, you and Baby Bop can stay here and watch for other ships," said Barney.

"Aye-aye!" said BJ.

"Me, me!" laughed Baby Bop.

"The rest of us can walk through the jungle to find help," said Barney.

Everyone had fun hiking through the jungle. There were lots of colorful butterflies and sweet-smelling flowers. The air was filled with the sounds of singing birds and chattering monkeys.

Finally, Barney and his friends found a very funny-looking house. It was painted with bright happy-looking colors and had a roof made of dried grass.

"Maybe there's someone inside who can help us," said Shawn.

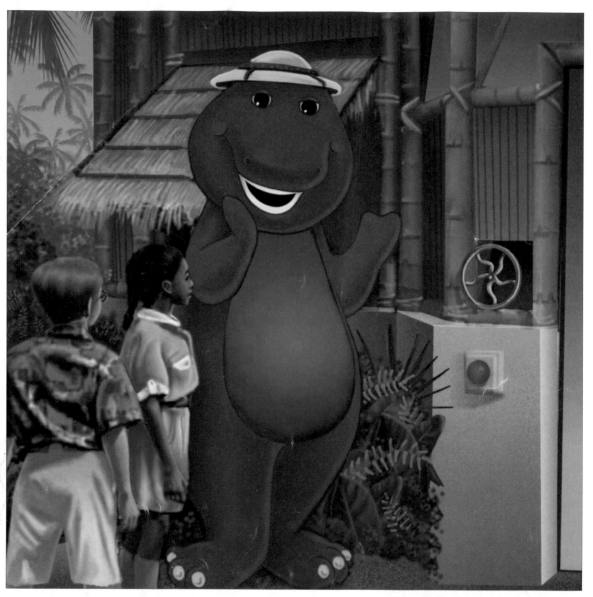

Barney turned a little crank by the door and everyone laughed when it made jack-in-the-box music! Just as the music finished, a little door popped open.

"Hello!" said the man inside. "Welcome to Imagination Island."

"My name is Professor Tinkerputt," said the man. "I invent all sorts of wonderful toys."

But the professor wouldn't let anyone play with the toys.

"Sorry," said the professor. "I came to this island because I don't like to share."

Barney asked Professor Tinkerputt if he could help get the ship out of the trees.

"No, I can't," the professor said sadly. "I'm too busy trying to fix my balloon machine. It only needs one more part, but there's nothing on the island to make it work."

Then Tosha had a good idea. She took off her heart necklace and carefully put it into the balloon machine.

"Try it now," said Tosha.

He tried the machine, and it worked! Out came balloons of every size and color!

"Good things happen when you share!" said Barney.
Professor Tinkerputt decided to try sharing too. He
asked everyone to play with his wonderful toys.

"You're right, Barney," he laughed. "It's fun to share."

Professor Tinkerputt was so happy that he decided to
leave the island and share his toys with children everywhere.

"May I go with you on your ship?" he asked. "Now I know
how to get it out of the trees!"

Professor Tinkerputt used his balloon machine to make lots of giant balloons that were tied to the ship. When there were almost too many balloons to count, the ship began to pull loose from the trees.

"Here we go!" said Barney as the ship went up...up...up into the air.

"We're flying!" giggled Baby Bop.

"Just like birds!" laughed BJ as he flapped his arms up and down.

Everyone cheered as the ship made one last circle around the island, then turned out over the blue ocean to head for home.

With Barney at the wheel, the ship sailed on and on until the sunset sky had become a sea of twinkling stars.

"It's a bee-yutiful night for flying," Barney said happily as he steered around a puffy white cloud.

"You'll be home soon," Professor Tinkerputt said to Tosha.
He smiled and gave her heart necklace back to her.
"Don't you need it anymore?" she asked.
"I can make another," he said. "Besides, you already
gave me a special gift. You taught me how to share again."
Tosha gave Professor Tinkerputt a very big hug.

"It looks like we're almost home," Barney called to his friends.

BJ and Baby Bop waved good-bye, then disappeared in a colorful burst of sparkles.

All of the children gave Barney a hug and thanked him for the wonderful adventure.

"It was fun for me too," Barney chuckled.

A little while later Tosha and Min tiptoed down the ship's stairway and back into Tosha's bedroom. There, sitting on Tosha's bed, was the little toy dinosaur.

"Barney?" both girls asked in surprise.

They turned around to look at the ship's stairway...but it was gone.

"I guess it really is time for bed," said Min with a big yawn.

"I think so too," said Tosha.

Tosha picked up Barney and carried him back to his place by the window.

"Thanks again, Barney," she whispered sleepily. She gave him one last squeeze, then went to bed.

Tosha and Min fell asleep right away, both dreaming happy dreams of their trip to Imagination Island. High in the night sky, a beautiful ship hanging from a cloud of balloons glided silently across the face of the moon. But no one saw it.

No one...except Barney.

2249018

2249